THE MUDDLE - HEADED WOMBAT IS VERY BAD

RUTH PARK

Illustrated by Noela Young

Angus & Robertson Publishers

Once in Big Bush it rained and it rained.

The first day was fun for the Muddle-headed Wombat and his best friend Mouse and their second-best friend Tabby Cat.

They kept looking out the windows and saying how lucky they were to have a cosy dry house.

"Of course," said Tabby, who was conceited, "*I* deserve it. How shocking if a super-pussy like me had to live in a leaky old tree like a possum or a koala."

"And Tab, another thing, Tab," said Wombat happily, "we have a loverly kind little Mouse who'll make a hugeous pile of sandwiches if we're good, won't you, Mouse, eh?"

Mouse *was* kind. Off it went gaily and made sandwiches, fish ones for Tabby and tomato for Wombat and a very small mosquito sandwich for itself. So they had an inside picnic.

It was so comfortable that Tabby and Wombat almost longed for a flood. But Mouse hoped and hoped that the next day it would be fine. It knew how growly and bristly wombats get when they're kept inside. It dreaded the awfulness of a cat with muddy paws.

However, on the first day everything was all right.

On the second day Wombat turned out his playbox and found lots of toys he had forgotten, and was pleased to meet again. Mouse read its

new library book, *Jennifer Mouse and the Ghost Rat*, which was very exciting. Tabby tried on all his smart clothes and admired himself.

"You gorgeous creature, you," he told himself. "I can hardly look at you without sunglasses."

"Never mind *that*," said Mouse rather sharply. "Show us how clever you are by reading us a story."

Tabby was charmed to be able to show off. He read his friends *The Wizard of Oz*, and although Wombat got muddled between lizards and wizards, and interrupted in the most annoying way, Tabby kept his temper.

"It is nice that we're being so good," said Mouse gratefully.

On the third day Tabby and Wombat prowled around glaring at everything and saying rude things about wet weather. Mouse went on reading *Jennifer Mouse*, for it had just reached the place where Jennifer first met the glimmery ghost rat, and Mouse's whiskers were thrilling to the very roots. Tabby sulked. Wombat drearily practised standing on his head and fell over.

"I do believe my tail's horribubbly bent," he complained.

"Oh, goody," said Tabby, cheering up. "Now I can play clever Doctor Tabby."

"You can play being an old fur coat, that's what," growled Wombat, hanging Tabby on a nail behind the kitchen door.

"Now, now," squeaked Mouse. "None of that. You ought to be ashamed, Wombat. Just when I was going to cook us some pancakes, too!"

But the pancakes settled things down only for a little while. Tabby scratched Wombat and Wombat sat on Tabby, and Mouse bit both of them. Wombat rolled away in a huff and had a fight with his teddybear. Then he was sorry, and took off his hat and cried some miserable tears into it.

"I'm awfullous, Tedda, treely ruly," he apologised. "But it was that terribubble cat that started it all. Let's go and throw him in the bath!"

"Oh, my," sighed Mouse. It scuttled off to its bedroom and listened sadly to the splashes, squalls, and the squoggy bleats from Tedda, who had fallen into the bath as well. Things crashed, doors slammed. And all the time the rain came down, more and more heavily.

Mouse's glasses misted over. "I just know they're going to ask for my jigsaw to play with," it whispered.

Mouse's jigsaw was special. Mouse's favourite cousin, Mousette, had given it to Mouse as a bedroom carpet. The picture on the jigsaw was of a fairy cottage with crooked chimneys and a goblin door-knocker. Mouse loved to walk around looking at the magic garden and pretending that it lived in the cottage all alone and had people like cats and wombats to visit only on birthdays and at Christmas.

Just then in flew Tabby. He had a bright blue nose and large spectacles drawn on with chalk.

"Goodness," said Mouse with surprise. "I thought you'd be sopping wet, Tabby dear."

"And I suppose you're disappointed that I'm not," said Tabby bitterly. "Oh, why are people so mean to cats? Why? Why?"

He preened. "If you must know, Meouse, I'm *not* wet because *I* pushed Wombat into the bath first. That's why he drew on my face with chalk.My handsome looks are ruined for life,I wouldn't be surprised."

"Oh, rubbish!" snapped Mouse. It marched out to make sure that Wombat wasn't dripping on too many things. It was very short with him, too. Tabby and Wombat became very good all of a sudden.

"You know, Meouse," said Tabby, "we're squabbling because we have nothing interesting left to do except you-know-what."

"No," said Mouse.

Even Wombat knew what you-know-what was.

"That loverly loverly jogsaw in Mouse's room," he said.

"No!" shouted Mouse.

"But we'll be so careful, we'll be angels," said Tabby.

"Treely ruly," coaxed Wombat. "Please, please, dear nice Mouse, my bestest friend in the whole world."

"And the prettiest," cooed Tabby.

And so, somehow, poor Mouse found itself lending its precious jigsaw to its friends.

It was true, they were wonderfully careful.

"Would you mind passing me that green piece that looks like a worm, horribubbly handsome old Tab?"

"Here you are, Wombat. Be careful now, because you know how much Meouse loves its jigsaw. And, if you've finished with it, Wombat, I'd rather like that brown three-cornered bit."

Mouse sighed with relief. Thankfully it crept away and took up *Jennifer Mouse and the Ghost Rat*. Jennifer was a fearless, adventurous mouse, just the kind Mouse itself would have loved to be. Its whiskers had just started to tingle again when a fearful commotion came from the

living-room. Mouse squeaked and scampered in to see what was happening. Wombat was lying on the floor pounding his feet. Tabby was looking haughty and smug.

"He's taken all the interesting bits," roared Wombat. "All I've got are hidjus blue squiggles that won't fit anywhere."

"But those are bits of sky, Wombat," explained Mouse.

"How terrible it must be to be a muddle-head, Meouse," said Tabby. "Just look, he's got the door of the cottage and he doesn't even *know*."

"It isn't, it isn't!" yelled Wombat.

"But there's a knob on it," said Tabby impatiently. "Where do you find knobs except on house doors, you muddle-head?"

At once Wombat clonked Tabby between the ears with a large piece of sky, and made a knob that was not on a door. Mouse was shocked to its toenails.

"To think," it said coldly, "how I've tried and tried to bring you up properly, Wombat!" Then it roared: "Be *quiet*, Tabby, you big crybaby! I can't hear myself squeak!"

"Cruel Meouse," snivelled Tabby. "I was just trying to tell you what Wombat is doing now, that's all."

Mouse could hardly believe its glasses. Its pink nose turned snow white. Wombat was grabbing bits of Tabby's end of the jigsaw and cramming them into his mouth.

"There goes the cow!" screeched Tabby. "There goes the garden gate!"

"Yes, and they tasted horribubble too," said Wombat. "Oooh, blah, yuk!"

"That was my very favourite thing," said Mouse in a trembling voice. "My cousin gave it to me for my third birthday, and besides that I loved it very much, and I used to make up imaginations about it, and the sky's broken, and there isn't any cow, and the flowers are all in bits and. . . ."

It gave a sob which was really very large for so small a mouse, and stumbled away and hid in the sugar bowl, pulling the lid on after itself. It heard Wombat fighting Tabby, and both of them blaming each other, but it was too broken-hearted to care. The end of its tail grew soggy from wiping its eyes. For Mouse was not fond of wet weather either, and it hated being inside the house for days and days. It had done all a mouse could do to keep its friends happy.

"I even made pancakes," sniffled Mouse. It rested its head on a sugar lump, but that was sharp-cornered and uncomfortable. "I'm a worn-out Mouse, that's what I am."

Softly a paw scratched the lid of the sugar bowl and Tabby cooed: "Please come out, Meouse."

"Because I've got splinters in my tongue, Mouse. It's terribubble to have splinters in your tongue, and all I did was to eat that silly old jogsaw," complained Wombat.

Mouse's glasses shot fire. It jumped out on the table.

"I don't care if your tongue bristles with splinters. Serve you right, you mean Wombat. And you're just as bad, Tabby Cat. I'm not going to squeak a word to you two for the rest of the day, so there."

Wombat stuck his lip out. Tabby tried to squeeze a tear into his cunning green eye. Mouse marched away, sat down in its red velvet armchair, which had come out of a dolls' house, and calmly began to read *Jennifer Mouse*. But it was very hard for Mouse.

Tabby and Wombat sat down and stared without a blink.

"Look, Wombat," whispered Tabby. "Mouse has its little mouth buttoned up as tight as tight."

"I can't see any buttons, Tab. Show me, Tab."

Mouse read on quietly, but it didn't see a word. Half of it wanted to giggle at Wombat, and the other half felt very offended and upset. It stared at the picture of Jennifer Mouse whacking the ghost rat on the head with an umbrella and wished it, too, always knew the right thing to do.

"Aw, I know, Tab," said Wombat. "If Mouse hasn't any buttons on its mouth, it must have a zipper."

"Let's have a teeny look," purred Tabby. He carefully lifted Mouse's top lip and stared at its pearly teeth. Oh, what a temptation for Mouse to bite his paw to the bone. But instead it quietly turned a page.

Foiled, its friends went into the corner of the room and had a whispered conversation.

"Plotting and planning," boiled Mouse, not seeing a word of the exciting paragraph where Jennifer Mouse felt the ice-cold claws of the ghost rat on the back of her neck. And it hardened its heart against its friends.

However, it was puzzled when they scurried into the kitchen. Very soon they came back with a tin of golden syrup.

"Oh, Meouse dear," cried Tabby dramatically. "Wombat is going to pour the golden syrup all over himself. Do stop him, Meouse, he's such a silly sausage!"

"Not as silly as you," chuckled wicked Wombat, as he poured the golden syrup all over Tabby.

Mouse put down *Jennifer Mouse*. It looked at Wombat with eyes like icicles. Wombat felt his whiskers crisp. Mouse looked at sticky Tabby, and the horrid pool of golden syrup on the floor.

"Very well then," it said, and its voice was colder than its eyes.

It took its matchbox suitcase from the wardrobe. Tabby's whiskers drooped. Wombat's heart sank like a stone.

"Wh-what are you doing with your suitcase, Mouse?" he quavered.

"I'm leaving home," said Mouse. "I shall go and live with my cousin Mousette."

Life without a mouse! The idea made Wombat tug his hat over his face and bawl. Tabby gave him a wicked pinch.

"It's all your fault, Wombat. Who painted my nose blue and ate the jigsaw and poured golden syrup on me?"

"I did, too," gulped Wombat. "I was treely ruly awfullous."

"So was that cat there!" said Mouse sternly.

Tenderly it put into the suitcase its pink satin ballet slippers, its dearest treasures next to the jigsaw. It was then that Tabby realised that

Mouse meant what it said. It was leaving. It was leaving its only cat — a beautiful, brainy, in all ways charming cat — to the mercies of a wombat who could only count to four, had fights with his teddybear, and sat on people until they were almost flattened. A wombat who thought rock-cakes had real rocks in them, and — here Tabby put a skinny little paw over his eyes with horror. He sucked in his cheeks so that he should look starved and friendless and in need of the guiding paw of a mouse.

"We need you, Meouse!"

"We love you so terribubbly, Mouse, treely ruly," quavered Wombat.

Mouse's heart ached for Wombat. It didn't ache so much for Tabby, who was rolling up his eyes and pretending to faint. But it felt it had to be firm.

"If you did love me so much you'd be better behaved," said Mouse. "Good-bye, all." And it picked up its suitcase and marched out of the

house. The rain had stopped but the wind was chill. Mouse came back.

"There, I knew you couldn't tear yourself away from your brilliant pussy," cried Tabby gladly.

"I came back for my cap and woolly coat, thank you *very* much, Tabby Cat," replied Mouse. It marched out again.

Tabby and Wombat had forgotten all their disagreements. They stood close together holding paws in a room which seemed lonely and dreary now that Mouse had gone.

"Mousette lives on the other side of Big Bush," said Tabby. "And it's getting dark, and in the dark there are mopokes and all kinds of bad things for meouses without cats and wombats to look after them."

They hurried after Mouse, but it had already vanished into the long shadows of Big Bush.

"Wahhhhhhh!" Wombat fell down in the mud and made noises of fright and misery. Tabby, who didn't care for mud, climbed up on Wombat's stomach and wailed. But this time he wasn't acting or pretending.

"We *were* bad, Wombat, and it's no wonder Meouse doesn't want to live with us. Now, be quiet, and let me think."

Wombat stopped roaring and looked hopeful. "Yes, you're terribubbly clever, old Tab. You think, that's right. Are you thinking, Tab? I can't hear your brains chugging. Because we can't let our loverly Mouse walk around Big Bush in the dark. Imaginabubble!"

In spite of all the noise Wombat was making, Tabby *was* thinking. He bounded off Wombat's stomach and said briskly, "Captain Tabby has decided. We shall go after that Meouse and no matter how much it squeaks and kicks and even bites, we shall bring it home.''

"Oh, Tab, you *are* clever!" Wombat's eyes shone with so much admiration that Captain Tabby felt a positive tiger.

"And because mopokes like tasty bits of cat as well as meouses, and for all I know, a nibble of wombat now and then, for they're not as fussy as cats, for instance —''

"We'll wear helmets!" cried Wombat.

Captain Tabby frowned. "I was going to say that. Don't interrupt.''

"Aw right, Captain Tabby," said Wombat humbly. "I'll just go and fetch the saucepans. For the helmets. Oh, Tabby, you are brainy. You must have brains you haven't even used yet.''

Tabby was still thinking about that when Wombat ambled back with the helmets. There was a small milk saucepan for Tabby and a round metal mixing basin for Wombat. The handle of Tabby's helmet kept slipping around to the front and falling down on his nose, but Tabby felt that was better than being pecked by a mopoke.

Meanwhile, what was happening to Mouse? It was very jumpy, and sorry that it had ever thought of running away from home. Night birds were awakening in the treetops. They stretched their wings and sharpened their beaks on twigs and bark and called to each other with harsh sad calls. Mouse heard the wings flutter and the beaks clack and grind and it trembled.

"If only my dear Mousette didn't live so far away! If only I had waited until tomorrow! If only I were fearless and daring like Jennifer Mouse!"

It crept under a mushroom to have a cry. But the mushroom was clammy and smelt unaired, and Mouse crept out again. It polished its glasses and glared around at the dark spooky bush.

"I *can* be like Jennifer Mouse if I try. I *will* go to live with Mousette."

But a tear ran down its nose.

"Oh, my, I do hope Wombat makes proper dinners for himself and that when he gets a prickle in his paw Tabby can get it out without hurting him. And I hope he isn't too 1-lonely at night times. . . ."

From away up a tree came an angry squawk and Mouse flickered back under the mushroom, its heart thumping.

"Who's that sneaking around down there? Squeak up, or I'll drop a cake on you!"

"Oh, what a relief!" whispered Mouse, who knew the cranky voice of Mrs Koala. She was a very unfriendly old lady even on fine days, and now she was even worse.

"It's only me, Mouse, Mrs Koala," cried Mouse, and it added rather proudly: "Guess what? I'm running away from home!"

"Never heard such twaddle in my life," shouted Mrs Koala. "Go home at once!"

Mouse's nose and ears turned bright red. "I'll run away any time I feel like it, thank you very much," it squeaked, and at once there was a perfect rain of cakes which crashed around it like stones, for Mrs Koala was the worst cook in Big Bush. Mouse ran as fast as it could. It dodged all the cakes but it fell in a hole.

"Bother, bother!" shouted Mouse, by now not only afraid but in a bad temper as well. The hole was much too deep, and the sides too crumbly for it to climb out. Mouse's suitcase had burst open and all its belongings had fallen out. Mouse groped here and groped there, and at

last it found its glasses. The first thing it saw was two heads peering inquisitively over the edge of the hole. Mouse's heart beat hard, but in a moment it saw that the heads belonged to possums.

"Hello!" it cried gladly. "Please help me out of this hole!"

"Don't *you*," grunted one possum to its friend.

"Don't *you* either," said the other.

"Us won't," they said together.

"Silly things," said Mouse. "It's only me, Mouse, from Wombat's house."

The possums laughed rudely. "That mouse wouldn't never leave its wombat," one said. "You ain't a mouse, you're a rat."

"No, I think it's a furry bug," said the other possum.

"That's right, us thinks you're a furry bug," said its friend. Mouse heard them laughing all the way up a tree. It stamped around a bit, but really its spirits were very low.

"Suppose the rain starts again," it said to itself. "Suppose this hole has spiders."

Just then something soft tumbled down on it, and Mouse shrieked at the top of its voice. But it was not a spider, only one of its little ballet slippers which had stuck on a root at the side of the hole and suddenly fallen. Mouse was glad to have its slipper. It clutched it tightly and tried not to be frightened. But that was hard.

"I can hear mysterious sounds," it whispered. And it *could*.

The sounds were crackles and grunts, and mutters, and thumps. They came closer and closer, and Mouse's teeth chattered.

Now dim moonlight lit Big Bush. It was soft and gauzy, broken into strange shadows and shapes by treetops and the last of the rain clouds. It sifted down through the leaves. It shone on Mouse's spectacles as poor Mouse stared upwards at the edge of the hole.

Suddenly Mouse saw an amazing thing. The head of a very strange animal peered over the edge. It was silvery, and had one long horn right in the middle of its forehead like a unicorn. Mouse put its paws over its spectacles and sank to the ground. Not even Jennifer Mouse, it felt, could bear looking at so scary a sight.

Now Wombat and Tabby had not enjoyed their walk through Big Bush. Tabby felt more delicate than he ever had before. He felt the proper place for so refined a cat was in bed, with a hot water bottle. But because he was the leader of the expedition he had to give a good example.

"Don't be frightened, Wombat. Brave Captain Tabby will look after you," he said.

"Aw, I'm not frightened, Tab, because wombats are night animals. Wombats like dark nights and mud and beetles and—"

"You might pretend," said Tabby bitterly. "Some people have no feelings at all. How can I be a hero cat if you won't be frightened so I can say don't be frightened, Tabby's here?"

Wombat was just going to say he'd do his best to be scared when Tabby reeled backwards. The handle of his helmet swung around and clanged Wombat on his mixing basin.

"If that's being a hero, it's very uncomfortabubble for me, treely ruly," complained Wombat. "So you just stop and be your usuabubble cowardly self, see?"

Tabby held tightly to Wombat's stout paw. "There's a hole in the track in front of us," he whispered, "and I looked in, and there were two terrible shining eyes, Wombat, and then they winked out. Oh, what a thing for a delicate pussy to see. I'm going to faint, I know I am."

When Mouse heard above it the voices of its very own dear (though wicked) friends, it gave such a cheer. Tabby shot up Wombat's arm and wound himself around his neck like a scarf.

"I do believe, Tab," said Wombat, beginning to bounce quietly with joy, "that's my Mouse down in that hole."

"Oh, it is, it is, dear, *dear* Wombat!" shrieked Mouse. Wombat felt around in the hole and fairly soon came upon a familiar, furry little bobble. He lifted it out tenderly, not noticing that Tabby had tipped into the hole, helmet and all.

"There you are, Mouse, eh? Treely ruly?"

Mouse just hugged Wombat, at least as far as its tiny arms would reach.

"Why are you wearing the mixing basin on your head, Wombat?" it asked. Wombat explained that the mixing basin was really a helmet to keep off the mopokes.

"And Tabby wore the milk saucepan. Oh, now I remember, he hopped down into that hole. He does some terribubbly strange things, Mouse. Perhaps it's because he's so clever."

Mouse peered into the hole. Pale moonlight showed Tabby sulking in a corner. Wet leaves drifted down on him.

"Aw," said Wombat, pleased. "He's just like a Bub in the Woods. Let's help, Mouse."

He grabbed a large armful of leaves and tossed them down on Tabby. Tabby made a noise like a boiling kettle. Yet kind little Mouse knew that he was a wet, cold, frightened cat.

"Please let's go home," it begged. "I'm so sleepy and hungry. You can see in the dark, Tabby, so please find all my things and put them back in the suitcase."

"Yes, and hurry up, you hidjus animal," ordered Wombat. "I never saw such a cat for sitting in the mud. Mouse wants to go home and make us some more pancakes, don't you, Mouse, eh?"

Mouse's spectacles began to glitter. But happy bouncing Wombat, and Tabby, climbing joyfully from the hole, did not notice.

"I'll be able to go off to Mousette in the morning," said Mouse cheerfully. "That's much more sensible."

Tabby choked. Wombat gave a great roar.

"But you're coming home to stay, Meouse!"

"We need you horribubbly much!"

"Oh, someone else will look after you and cook pancakes," said Mouse cheerily. "Why don't you ask Mrs Koala?"

"Mrs Koala is the worsest cook in Big Bush!" said Wombat.

"I heard that, you fat muddle-headed lump!" came a harsh voice from the bluegum. "Take that!"

Rock-cakes rained down like hail. Mouse flashed under Wombat's mixing basin. Tabby darted around the other side of his stout friend, who just stood there muttering while the rock-cakes bounced off him.

"Tomorrow," promised Wombat, "Tabby Cat and I are going to come along and chew your gumtree down, you cranky old koala lady."

"Oh, no, Wombat," said Tabby, looking as much like an angel as he could. "That would be bad, and you know we promised each other never to be bad again, as long as our Meouse came back to live with us."

Wombat stuck his lip out. "Going to be horribubbly boring being good every day. Not very excitabubble for poor Mouse, I must say."

"Wouldn't you like us to be just a little wicked now and then, Meouse?" asked Tabby in his most charming voice. "Just for fun, Meouse?"